Written by
Sam McBratney

Illustrated by
Sam Usher

The
MOST-LOVED
BEAR

Some teddy bears are young and some are not so young;
but only a very few are as old as the bear in this story.

MACMILLAN CHILDREN'S BOOKS

Fifty years ago, or maybe sixty years ago,
a little girl called Mary Rose bought a
teddy bear with the sixpences she had
saved in her moneybox.

Mary Rose loved the look in her teddy's big brown eyes
and the feel of his soft fur. She called her new bear "Growly Bear"
because he growled when she tipped him up.

Her mummy sewed a G on the bottom
of one foot and a B on the bottom of the other.

Growly Bear became
a very special friend
and went everywhere
with Mary Rose.

Then one sad day,
Mary Rose lost him
on a train.

She tried to find him – but Growly Bear ended up
in the Lost Property Office, hidden behind all
the lost umbrellas, hats and gloves.

"Someone is sure to come for me soon," Growly Bear may have said
to himself, trying to look on the bright side – but no one did.

No one came for him until that blowy day in autumn when everything in the Lost Property Office was put up for sale, and Growly Bear was bought by a boy called Ronnie and his dad.

They thought that he was very cheap – a bargain bear, in fact. And that's what they called him: Bargain Bear.

There wasn't much room in Ronnie's house for toys, so his new Bargain Bear got a bit squashed and a bit bashed.

Bargain Bears are tough, though, and they don't mind a bit of squashing and bashing.

Besides, Ronnie loved reading, and he read many a story to his good friend Bargain Bear.

After some years had gone by, Ronnie's dad had to make room for different things – Ronnie was growing up fast …

… and needed room for his record-player and his books – so he sold Bargain Bear to the second-hand shop.

"Someone is sure to come for me," Bargain Bear
may have thought to cheer himself up.

But it isn't easy to look on the bright side when you've lost
your growl, and you're not the brand new bear you used to be.

How long was he there in
the second-hand shop?
It might have been years,
for Bargain Bears are not
good at knowing the time.
Then one day, he was spotted
by twin brothers, and they
bought him!

Living with brothers
who love football
can be rough.

One unlucky day, while kicking
their ball in the house, they
broke one of their mother's
flying ducks and had the ball
taken away from them.

Bargain Bear soon
became the ball!

Before long those twins
broke another duck.
Their mum marched
them straight to bed . . .

. . . and gave
Bargain Bear to
a man who came
collecting for
a charity shop.

Sitting in the charity shop, Bargain Bear may have worried that no one would want him. How can you look on the bright side when you've lost your growl and you've got a loose eye and there are holes in your body where the stuffing shows through?

Then a girl called Veronica saw him and loved him at once!
She brought him home that same day because he was very,
very cheap – cheap enough to buy with her pocket money.

Veronica gave Bargain Bear a bath and a good brush.

She set him up high where he could not be chewed or thrown about, for Veronica had small brothers and sisters who often broke her toys. Then, when night-time came, Veronica would lift down her Bargain Bear for a cuddle.

One morning her sisters found him under the covers of her bed.
They had a tug-of-war with Bargain Bear – they pulled
and pulled until one of his arms came off!

Poor Bargain Bear, but what could they do with him now? "Mummy, don't just throw him out!" cried Veronica. "No, of course I won't throw him out, we'll give him to the toy hospital," said her mother. And they did.

TOY
REPAIR

How long did Bargain Bear sit in the back of the toy mender's shop? No one knows. He may have wished for a boy or girl to take him home, but a bear with a torn arm?

Even someone who tried to look on
the bright side can't have been too hopeful
that such a thing would happen.

At last, however, the
toy mender got busy
with needle, thread
and buttons.

He sewed the arm
back on; did a patch
here; put a patch there,

until he looked at
Bargain Bear and said …

"As good as new!"

That was a bit of an exaggeration, but Bargain Bear certainly looked much improved. He even had a new growly voice, which must have pleased him a lot. When you tipped him forward, his growl was as grand as it had ever been.

The toy mender sold Bargain Bear to an antiques shop,
a shop full of old and very expensive things.

Bargain Bear may have wondered who would
buy him, for this was not the sort of shop that
children usually came into.

But then came the week before Christmas.
The street outside sparkled under a host of many-coloured
lights, and the shoppers hurrying by hardly seemed to notice
the flakes of snow falling from a black sky.
A lady and her husband came to an antiques shop.

The lady glanced up at the teddy bear
in the window, then looked again.
The second time she noticed
a G on his right foot.

"Oh my goodness!" she said.
"It couldn't be . . . could it?"

"Let's go in and look at the other foot, Mary Rose," said her husband, who had often heard the story of Growly Bear and how he had the letter G on one foot and B on the other.

"It's there – the B!" cried Mary Rose. "It's him, my Growly Bear! After all these years he's mine again – I wonder where he's been? Isn't this a fine thing!"

It was a very fine thing. Mary Rose paid one
hundred pounds to the shopkeeper and
took her Growly Bear home.
"This time I'm not going to lose you,"
she told him.

And she didn't. He still lives with Mary Rose,
and I should think he's pleased, don't you?

After all, it's not so hard to look on the bright
side when someone loves you as much as that.

For Ben – S.U.

The story 'Bargain Bear' first published in the collection
In the Light of the Moon in 2001

This picture book edition published 2018
by Macmillan Children's Books
an imprint of Pan Macmillan
20 New Wharf Road, London N1 9RR
Associated companies throughout the world
www.panmacmillan.com

ISBN (MME): 978-1-5098-5429-5
ISBN (OME): 978-1-5290-0209-6

1 3 5 7 9 8 6 4 2

A CIP catalogue record for this book is available from the British Library.
Printed in China